D0103626

WARNING!

THIS BOOK HAS LOADS OF VERY DISGUSTING MONSTERS IN IT!

Hairy ones, smelly ones, fat ones, oozy ones. None of them are very nice, and they study the Monsterbook to become more not very nice.

Monsterbook is written by monsters, for monsters. A filthy, fact-packed handbook to everything monster!

Michael Broad spent much of his childhood gazing out of the window imagining he was somewhere more interesting. Now he's a grown-up, Michael still spends a lot of time gazing out of the window imagining he's somewhere more interesting – but these days he writes and illustrates books as well.

Books by Michael Broad

MONSTERBOOK: PONGDOLLOP
AND THE SCHOOL STINK
MONSTERBOOK: SNOTGOBBLE
AND THE BOGEY BULLY

JAKE CAKE: THE FOOTBALL BEAST
JAKE CAKE: THE PIRATE CURSE
JAKE CAKE: THE ROBOT DINNER LADY
JAKE CAKE: THE SCHOOL DRAGON
JAKE CAKE: THE VISITING VAMPIRE
JAKE CAKE: THE WEREWOLF TEACHER

MONSTERBOOK

Pongdollop
and the
School Stink

MICHAEL BROAD

PUFFIN

PUFFIN BOOKS

Published by the Penguin Group
Penguin Books Ltd, 80 Strand, London WC2R 0RL, England
Penguin Group (USA) Inc., 375 Hudson Street, New York, New York 10014, USA
Penguin Group (Canada), 90 Eglinton Avenue East, Suite 700, Toronto, Ontario,
Canada M4P 2Y3 (a division of Pearson Penguin Canada Inc.)
Penguin Ireland, 25 St Stephen's Green, Dublin 2, Ireland (a division of Penguin Books Ltd)
Penguin Group (Australia), 250 Camberwell Road, Camberwell, Victoria 3124, Australia
(a division of Pearson Australia Group Pty Ltd)
Penguin Books India Pvt Ltd, 11 Community Centre, Panchsheel Park,
New Delhi – 110 017, India
Penguin Group (NZ), 67 Apollo Drive, Rosedale, North Shore 0632, New Zealand
(a division of Pearson New Zealand Ltd)
Penguin Books (South Africa) (Pty) Ltd, 24 Sturdee Avenue, Rosebank,
Johannesburg 2196, South Africa

Penguin Books Ltd, Registered Offices: 80 Strand, London WC2R 0RL, England

puffinbooks.com

First published 2009
1

Copyright © Michael Broad, 2009
All rights reserved

The moral right of the author/illustrator has been asserted

Set in Perpetua
Made and printed in England by Clays Ltd, St Ives plc

Except in the United States of America, this book is sold subject to the condition that it shall
not, by way of trade or otherwise, be lent, re-sold, hired out, or otherwise circulated without
the publisher's prior consent in any form of binding or cover other than that in which it is
published and without a similar condition including this condition being imposed on the
subsequent purchaser

British Library Cataloguing in Publication Data
A CIP catalogue record for this book is available from the British Library

ISBN: 978-0-141-32453-1

CONTENTS

FLESHBLOB DETAILS

NAME ....Will..........

ADDRESS ..33 Highland Road..

this book belongs to URK

MONSTERBOOK

· — · — ·

WELCOME TO THE REVOLTING WORLD
OF THE MONSTERBOOK! THE GRISLY
GUIDE TO ALL THINGS MONSTER!

Whether you're hideously hairy,
terrifyingly tentacled, creepily clawed or
just a great big mess of disgustingness,
Monsterbook has everything you need for
a career in fear.

This book comes with the name and
address of your allocated fleshblob
FOR SCARE-TRAINING PURPOSES!

THIS IS URK
Urk is a monster.
But to his parents'
disappointment he's
not very scary.

When Urk began scare training with the
MONSTERBOOK he made friends with
Will, his allocated fleshblob!

THIS IS WILL
Will is a human.
He thinks monsters are
revolting, but also very
interesting.

SCARE TRAINING
When Urk's meant to be out scaring Will,
the pair watch TV, eat snacks and read
the MONSTERBOOK.
Urk makes up weekly scare reports for his
parents, and Will learns more about
the disgusting world of
Monsterland.

MONSTERLAND

Monsterland is the underground world where monsters live. It's very dirty, smelly and lit by thousands of stolen light bulbs.

Earthy tunnels lead to the human world above, where monsters enter through secret doorways – hidden under beds, behind curtains and inside wardrobes...

1
Urk and Will

Urk closed the *Monsterbook* and peered up at his parents.

'Scare them until they wee the bed?' he frowned. 'It just seems a bit *mean*.'

Urk's dad gave an angry snort and his mum fled the room in tears. It was the young monster's first night on scare training and his parents had hoped the *Monsterbook* would spark *some* enthusiasm.

It hadn't, but he didn't really have a choice.

Urk recently finished bottom of his class in Basic Boo, having displayed a wilful lack of menace. Now he'd graduated to solo scares his parents were determined to make a monster of him.

Clutching the *Monsterbook* and using the handy map provided, Urk trudged through the dark, earthy tunnels out of Monsterland until he found the wardrobe belonging to Will, his allocated fleshblob. He was about to scratch *ominously* on the door, as described in chapter one, when his hooves suddenly became tangled in a bunch of wire hangers and he crashed into the room!

Then everything went dark.

When everything went light again, it went light blue – which was the colour of Will's bedroom. Looking around, Urk found the boy flicking through the *Monsterbook* with great interest.

'So, you're a monster?' Will asked cautiously.

'Um, yeah,' said Urk, sitting up to find himself wrapped in a woolly blanket.

'And I'm your allocated . . .' The boy ran a finger down the page until he found the right word. '. . . fleshblob?' he said with a frown.

The monster shrugged uncomfortably. This was followed by an awkward silence. The boy closed the book and drummed his fingers on the top, while the

monster fiddled with the corner of the
woolly blanket and wiggled his hooves.
Then Will rummaged in his pocket,
pulled out a small white bag and offered
it to Urk.

'Do you want a fizzy cola bottle?' he
asked.

From that night on, whenever Urk
was supposed to be on nightly scare
manoeuvres, the pair sat up watching TV,
eating crisps and reading the *Monsterbook*.
Urk made up elaborate scare stories to

tell his parents, while Will learned all about the disgusting world of monsters.

So everything worked out really well . . .

2
Will the Jub Jub

'BOO!' said Urk, jumping from the wardrobe and plonking his rucksack on Will's cluttered desk. The young monster was out of breath from running through the tunnels.

'ARGH!' said Will, glancing up from yesterday's *Nasty News*, Monsterland's nightly newspaper. 'What's up?'

'This!' said Urk, rolling out a messy, crumpled poster.

'An uprising?' said Will, sitting up straight. 'I thought monsters were happy

MONSTERS!

THE GREAT AND MIGHTY
PONGDOLLOP
WANTS VOLUNTEERS FOR
AN UPRISING AGAINST
FLESHBLOBS!

MEETING IN THE MONSTER
HALL ON THURSDAY AT
9 P.M.

FREE TEA AND
HAIRBALLS!

living underground. You said they only ever surface to scare people and steal light bulbs?'

'Monsters have never tried to take over the world before, it's far too clean up here,' said Urk. 'And we've only survived this long underground because grown-ups don't believe in us, which makes a monster uprising the worst idea *ever*!'

'What's a Pongdollop?' asked Will.

'That's probably his name,' said Urk, 'but I've never heard of him.'

Will glanced at his watch. 'The meeting's in an hour!'

'Yeah, we'd better hurry,' said Urk, quickly rolling up the poster. 'If we're going to stand any chance of stopping Pongdollop, we have to find out exactly what he's planning!'

'Us?' gasped Will, who was happy to learn about monsters from the safety of his room, but had no plans to *visit* Monsterland. Mostly because fleshblobs wouldn't get far before something bad happened to them.

'Oh, I've already thought about that and you can disguise yourself as a Jub Jub,' said Urk, pulling a brown sack and a pair of forks from his rucksack, thinking this would explain everything.

It didn't explain anything, so Will
grabbed the *Monsterbook* and flicked
through the 'J's in the 'Gruesome Gallery'
section. The 'Gruesome Gallery'
contains every kind of monster known
to monster, and eventually he found
a Jub Jub.

'Is *this* web-weave, breathable fabric?'
Will asked, picking up the dirty smelly
sack with the tips of his fingers.

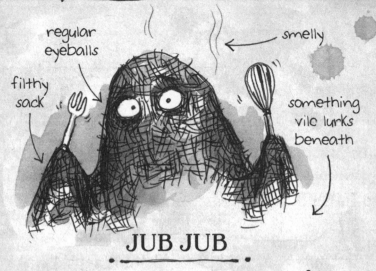

regular
eyeballs

smelly

filthy
sack

something
vile lurks
beneath

JUB JUB

Jub Jubs are the most disgusting of all
monsters and are forced by monster
law to stay covered at all times. To look
upon a Jub Jub would scare even the
most fearsome monster!

Jub Jubs can't even look at Jub Jubs, so
nesting females hatch their eggs in little
sacks because the sight of their own
revolting offspring would make them
scream and run away.

SACKS'R'US: Where the coolest Jub Jubs
buy web-weave, breathable fabrics!

'No,' said Urk. 'It's just a dirty, smelly sack.'

'And the forks?'

'You'll have to use them for hands,' Urk said, handing them over. 'Even the sight of a Jub Jub's hands would make a monster puke, so they have to use *implements*. Anyway, your pink ones would be a *dead* giveaway.'

'Are you sure this will work?' Will frowned, pulling the ragged sack over his head. He jabbed the forks through the material and shifted it

around until he was peering through two meshy eyeholes.

'Trust me,' said Urk, packing the book away and throwing the rucksack over his shoulder. '*No one* will want to lift that sack to find out what's underneath.'

Urk headed for the wardrobe and was about to enter the tunnels, when he noticed Will wasn't behind him.

The boy was still standing by the desk looking like a muddy ghost.

'It'll be fine!' said Urk. 'I promise.'

Will reluctantly shuffled through the hidden doorway of the wardrobe after his monster friend, bumping into a few things along the way until he got used to the sack and the smell of the tunnels.

A few odd-looking creatures scuttled past and Will tried not to stare or scream

or run in the opposite direction. He also
tried to look like a Jub Jub and not a
fleshblob draped in a sack.

3
Monster City

After many twists and turns through
reeking tunnels, Urk and Will eventually
stepped out into a giant underground
cavern with grubby light bulbs planted
in the ceiling like stars. The cavern was
the biggest hole Will had ever seen, but
it needed to be big because it had a
whole city in it!

Will decided Monster City was not
all that different from the city above,
except that this one was much darker,
smellier and looked as though it was made

of dung. Putrid oozefalls burped and
gurgled down the cavern walls and
a forest of giant fungus surrounded the
city like a demented fairy ring.

'YUCK!' said Will, pinching his nose
between two forks.

'Thanks,' said Urk, and set off down the
slimy cavern edge.

Will gazed, wide-eyed, as they made
their way through the fungus forest, past
the slug slums and into the city – where
the buildings towered over them like
enormous compost heaps. In the busy
streets he saw lots of unfamiliar creatures

SLUG SLUMS

Giant slugs are a monster's favourite food. Yummy and satisfyingly slimy, slug slums circle Monster City and are raided daily by slugpickers.

in all shapes and sizes, and made a mental note to look them up later in the *Monsterbook*. Others he recognized from the 'Gruesome Gallery', like Parpers, Quillylous and a couple of Big Ugly Jennies.

PARPER

Parpers are shaped like bagpipes and specialize in rude windy noises. The monsters' head is full of gas - so don't expect too much in the way of conversation.

QUILLYLOU

Quillylous are very shy and nervous, but don't mistake this for weakness. A startled Quillylou can scream loud enough to make bones vibrate and teeth fall out.

Particularly hazardous to Small Spiteful Jennies!

(see opposite page)

SMALL SPITEFUL JENNIE

• —————— •

Small Spiteful Jennies are a furious bundle of sharp gnashing teeth on tall bony legs. They are very rare, but extremely dangerous!

BIG UGLY JENNIE

• —————— •

This more common Jennie is a mass of tatty hair and has wide, staring eyes. Big Ugly Jennies are very sociable and will often spit on a stranger's head as a friendly 'Hello'.

As they made their way down Snot
Street, Will felt something wet and slimy
land on his head and looked up to see a
Big Ugly Jennie grinning down at him. He
waved a fork at it in what he hoped was
a friendly gesture, and then legged it to
catch up with Urk.

SNOT STREET
Monster City's busiest
trading district, where you
can buy anything from
dung pies to deep-fried flies.

DOG POO
Monsterland architects
often design buildings using
the mathematical rule
known as 'Perfect Brown'.
Perfect Brown is the most
pleasing shape to monster
eyes and is the exact shape
of a curly dog poo.

The young monster was standing
outside the mighty Monster Hall.

'It looks like a giant curly dog poo!'
said Will, gazing up at the big brown
dollop.

'Thanks!' said Urk, and led them inside.

The interior of Monster Hall was exactly what Will imagined the inside of a giant curly dog poo might look like – curved brown walls, winding staircases and ploppy chandeliers.

'Now, leave all the talking to me,' Urk whispered as they entered the foyer.

A small ugly creature was holding a pile of leaflets. His most striking feature was the hump on his back – it was bigger than his body and looked like a giant walnut.

'Are you here for the great and mighty Pongdollop?' he asked suspiciously.

'Yes,' said Urk. 'Down with all fleshblobs!'

'Follow the slime trail to the main hall,'

the creature grumbled, handing Urk
a grubby leaflet. Then he screwed his
eyes shut and skewered another leaflet
blindly on to Will's
left fork. 'Tea and
hairballs will be
served afterwards.'

'That thing didn't

MONSTER TEA

Hot drink made from
bogbeetle droppings.

look at me once,' Will whispered as
they followed the slime trail down a low
brown corridor towards the main hall.
'Which is rich considering he was
a walking hump!'

'That was an Underling,' Urk
explained. 'Underlings aren't *technically*
monsters because they have no scary
bits or natural defences. They survive
by working for big monsters in return
for protection, and he didn't look at
you because he was frightened.'

'I'm a sack with cutlery!' said Will,
lifting his right fork and frowning at it.
'Unless he thought I might prick him in
the bum with one of these?'

'He was worried he might see
something *under* the sack,' said Urk.
'Most monsters are tough enough to

survive a glimpse of a Jub Jub, like a
bit of elbow or a toe. But that would be
enough to *kill* an Underling.'

'We could have fun with that,' Will
chuckled, peeping out from under the rag.

'If an Underling found out you were a
fleshblob, it could still pull your arms and
legs off and hit you over the head with
them,' warned Urk. 'They can be pretty
aggressive.'

'You just said they were defenceless!'
Will gasped, quickly throwing the sack
back down and adjusting the hem to
make sure nothing human was sticking
out.

'Defenceless to *monsters*,' Urk
corrected.

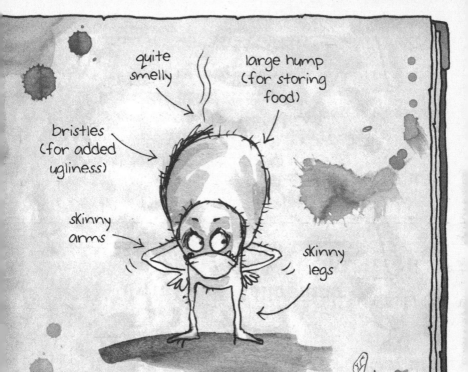

quite
smelly

large hump
(for storing
food)

bristles
(for added
ugliness)

skinny
arms

skinny
legs

UNDERLING
(TECHNICALLY NOT A MONSTER)

• — • — •

Underlings are the lowest of the low
in Monsterland. They are only tolerated
because they make themselves useful.
The ones who don't make themselves
useful are not tolerated, or alive
any more.

INTELLIGENCE: Underlings may not be
very scary, but they are smarter than
the average monster.

4

The Great and Mighty Pongdollop

At the opening of the main hall, Urk and
Will paused in the doorway and scanned
the room. There was a poor turnout for
the great and mighty Pongdollop, despite
the promise of free hairballs. Six monsters
were seated among a sea of chairs filling
half of the hall. The other half of the
hall was filled with the great and mighty
Pongdollop!

The monster was a sprawling mass of

spotty tentacles, but surprisingly nimble as he slithered behind the podium, mumbling angrily to himself. He seemed to be rehearsing his speech because two tentacles were flapping in tyrannical gestures, while the rest shuffled leaflets, flicked through notes and poured a glass of something that looked like water, but was yellow.

YELLOW WATER
Don't ask!

'He's huge!' squeaked Will as they
shuffled down the aisle and took their
seats.

The plan had been to go along to
the meeting and find a way to stop
Pongdollop's uprising — but at the
moment they were busy taking deep
breaths and trying not to run screaming
from the building.

Will plucked the
leaflet from his left
fork with his right
fork and held
it at eye level
with both
forks. He was
surprised at
how quickly he
had mastered
the forks because
he'd never got the
hang of chopsticks.

'It's not the
most *inspiring*
leaflet.' Will
frowned, secretly
hoping this

meant Pongdollop was a bit stupid and incapable of rousing a flock of panicky pigeons. 'Not to mention the really bad spelling.'

Urk was busy reading the description of an Octapongus in the *Monsterbook*. There was an illustration of something that looked like Pongdollop, but the scale of the drawing *really* didn't do him justice.

'Look at this,' he said. 'We should know exactly what we're up against!'

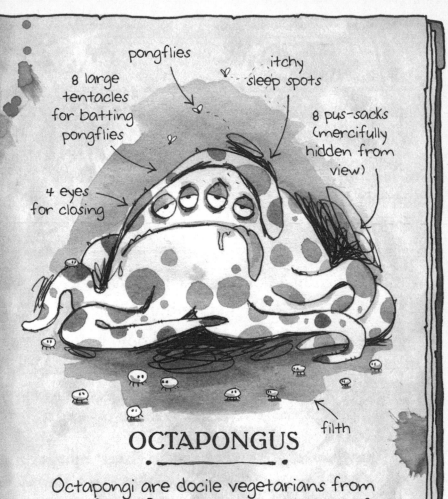

pongflies

itchy
sleep spots

8 large
tentacles
for batting
pongflies

8 pus-sacks
(mercifully
hidden from
view)

4 eyes
for closing

filth

OCTAPONGUS

Octapongi are docile vegetarians from
the Outer Regions who spend most of
their time in a very deep sleep. This
species is almost extinct as they're
too lazy to seek a mate.
The Octapongus is the least ambitious of
all monsters, and the least interesting!

😶 BOO BOO: Mites who feast on filth!

Will and Urk peered up at the fuming, growling mass of tentacles as it thumped the podium several times with its head, sending notes and leaflets into the air in a shower of paper.

'He doesn't look very docile,' said Will.

'No, he doesn't,' said Urk.

The Underling scuttled up the aisle, leapt on to one of Pongdollop's tentacles and scaled the side of his giant head. Perched on the lumpy summit he whispered something into a crusty hole and then scuttled back down again.

Pongdollop surveyed the gathering with a disappointed snarl while his assistant gathered the scattered notes and arranged them neatly on the podium. Then the Underling peeped over the top and addressed the hall.

'MONSTERS AND MONSTERS!' he yelled, arms outstretched for dramatic emphasis, which would have been more dramatic if he were not so small.

'I give you the great and mighty PONGDOLLOP!'

With this, Pongdollop slithered forward, swept the Underling across the stage with a swish of a tentacle and roared at the top of his voice. The noise made the room quake and the chairs clattered like nervous crabs.

The six monsters began clapping and whooping, so Urk joined in. Will felt a bit left out so he tapped his forks together

in a way he hoped looked enthusiastic
and not at all fleshblobby.

'SILENCE, SCUM!' roared
Pongdollop, waving his tentacles angrily
at the group.

The claps and whoops ended abruptly,
while Will's forks carried on tapping
like turbocharged knitting needles.
Urk had to nudge his friend with a swift
elbow to make him stop.

'I am the great and mighty Pongdollop!'
roared Pongdollop, four mad eyes
peering around the hall independently
of each other. 'And you are the most
hideous, disgusting, smelly bunch of
freaks it has ever been my displeasure
to witness!'

'HOORAY!' cheered the monsters,
because this was a bit of a compliment.

MONSTER COMPLIMENTS

Anything bad is good when complimenting monsters. Filthy, dirty, foul, revolting and putrid are all very acceptable.

You may remark upon the size, smelliness, spikiness and hairiness of a horn, tentacle or face. And insult a monster by saying these features are small, soapy, soft and patchy.

'YOU BIG UGLY FREAK, I LIKE YOU!'
Contains 100 popular compliments and is available from all good book stores!

5
Octapongus Rant

'Are you weary of living in the soap-
scented shadow of the puny fleshblobs
living above us?' boomed Pongdollop,
jabbing a tentacle into the dung ceiling
of the hall. 'Tired of creeping around
in tunnels and performing minor frights
and scares?' he added, rearing up and
wiggling his tentacles.

'YEAH!' chorused the crowd,
while Urk and Will exchanged worried
glances.

'Well, I am here today to tell you

about Stink Ink!' roared
Pongdollop, lifting a bottle
of black fluid from behind
the podium. 'Stink Ink
was manufactured in my
own whiffy pus-sacks and
is guaranteed to turn all
soapy-washed fleshblobs
into foul, filthy STINK
BOMBS!'

The crowd cheered
as the Underling
reappeared with a box
of small black bottles
and passed them out
among the monsters.
He handed two
bottles to Urk and
nodded that one was
for the Jub Jub.

'Once a suitable number have been
squirted,' Pongdollop continued, 'they

will roam the streets and spread their stink among others, dirtying the world above for monsters to live in. There will be *retching* and *puking*, and very soon everything will become one big cesspool of stink and sick –'

A claw shot up in the front row causing Pongdollop to lose the thread of his rant.

'WHAT?' he spat angrily.

'Um, what about those of us who lack the equipment to squirt the genius Stink Ink?' asked a thorny Crabby, tapping his armoured body to illustrate the absence of pus-sacks.

'You will be provided with my
own patented strap-on pus-sack with
adjustable nozzle!' growled Pongdollop,
waving a tentacle at the Underling,
who had reappeared with another box
containing leather balloons attached to a
series of complicated straps and nozzles.
The Underling distributed these to all but
a smug-looking Bulbous, who lifted its
arms to reveal two modest pit-pumps.

MONSTER INVENTIONS

•——————•

Monsters are very keen inventors, although their area of interest is mostly limited to scare appliances and accessories:

MOOF'S GROWLER

Box with 3 growls 'GR!' 'GRR!' and 'GRRR!'

SHADOW LANTERN

Projects large scary shadows on the wall.

THE SCRATCHER

Clockwork claws that create scratchy noises.

FLOWER DRILL

No one knows what this invention does.

The above inventions, along with many more, can be seen at Monster City's
SCARE MUSEUM!

Pongdollop continued to rant about a nauseating new world reeking of toe jam and fish poo, while Urk re-read the Octapongus description in the Monsterbook. The young monster was

certain he'd missed something. Pongdollop was definitely an Octapongus, so why was he so mean and motivated when he should have been a big lazy lump?

'. . . and the only thing left to decide is where to strike our first disgusting blow!'

roared Pongdollop. He pulled a cord and a large map tumbled down the wall behind him. 'Now, after giving this matter careful consideration —'

'St Margaret's Elementary School!' yelled Will, who was so wrapped up in the rant he'd forgotten who, what and where he was. Urk slammed the book shut and eyed his friend nervously.

'WHO SAID THAT?' Pongdollop demanded.

All heads turned to Will, who

swallowed hard and raised a quivering
fork.

Pongdollop leapt from the stage and
slithered towards the boy, his sheer bulk
shoving chairs sideways in a chorus of

shrieks, until he was bearing down on
the cowering bundle of rags.

'What is your name?' hissed Pongdollop,
his enormous mouth frothing with fury.

'Will,' squeaked Will, too terrified to
lie.

'WILL?' roared the Octapongus.

'Willijub,' Will added, after Urk nudged him.

'Well, Will Willijub,' growled Pongdollop, scratching his lumpy head. 'I think that is an EXCELLENT suggestion.' And he slithered back to the stage, his tentacles tidying the disrupted chairs behind him.

'St Margaret's Elementary School!'
roared Pongdollop, jabbing the map
with the tip of a tentacle. 'Easily located,
highly populated and with widespread
distribution when the smelly little
fleshblobs run home to their soapy
mumsie-wumsies!'

An enthusiastic cheer rose from the
crowd.

'We will gather at St Margaret's Elementary School tomorrow,' Pongdollop said, four eyes rolling around in concentration. 'At break time in the playground! When all the little fleshblobs are conveniently gathered for a Stink Ink squirt-a-thon!'

'HOORAY!' roared the hall.

'Now, please fill your ugly faces at my expense.' Pongdollop pointed to the back of the hall where the Underling was laying out paper cups and emptying bags of hairballs into bowls.

HAIRBALLS

Cats often spit their hairballs through hidden doorways. These are then gathered up from the tunnels, packaged, and sold to monsters as a delicious snack.

Chairs immediately scraped the floor
as the monsters stampeded towards
the buffet, pushing and shoving and
clambering over each other's heads.
Pongdollop exited the building through
an extra-large doorway behind the stage,
quickly followed by the Underling who
zigzagged to and fro holding a tottering
pile of boxes.

'What were you *thinking*?' whispered
Urk, tucking the book, the bottles and the

wobbly pus-sacks into his rucksack. 'For a moment there I thought we were going to end up as part of the buffet!'

'Sorry, I just got carried away with all the shouting!' Will gasped. 'But I do remember thinking that if he's going to take over the world anyway, I might as well get a day off school out of it.'

'We'll have to worry about that later,' said Urk, turning his head to the back of the hall where the monsters were ravaging the food. 'First we need to get hold of those bottles!'

6
Hairball Buffet Brawl

Urk and Will approached the buffet, where the six bottles of Stink Ink belonging to the monsters had been lined up along the table. The monsters were busy snuffling like pigs at a trough, so no one noticed when Urk slipped each bottle carefully into his rucksack.

'Now leave the talking to me this time,' said Urk, and disappeared under the filthy tablecloth.

Will was happy never to speak again. Or at least until he got back home, where

saying the wrong thing can get you into
trouble but rarely gets you eaten. A voice
suddenly boomed from beneath the table
with a barrage of complicated insults,
each in a different accent and strangely
monster-specific.

'Your pit-pumps are pathetic compared
to my ferocious spines!' was the first;
followed by, 'Call that a horn? I could
snip it off with one snap of my giant
claw!'; and finally, 'One eye? That's scary!
I've got ten and they're all more gooey
than yours!'

Around the table the feasting halved

as three monster heads slowly reared
up, glaring at the spines, eyes and claws
of the remaining monsters. The Bulbous
growled at the Spinula, the Horned Hilla
snarled at the Crabby, and the One-Eyed
Wig glared at the Deccapeep.

BULBOUS

The Bulbous is very fat and slimy, with underarm pit-pumps for squirting their own putrid pit-perfume!

SPINULA

The Spinula is covered in long sharp spines. If threatened, this monster will roll into a prickly, thistly ball!

HORNED HILLA

The Horned Hilla is a very short monster and tries to make up for this by growing a large elaborate head horn!

CRABBY

The Crabby has one large claw for snipping and a thorny armoured shell to protect the squidgy bits inside!

ONE-EYED WIG

One-Eyed Wigs are very hairy. Amid all the hair they have a massive gooey eyeball for giving menacing glares!

DECCAPEEP

Deccapeeps have ten eyes, four bunny ears and a mop of wiry hair. These monsters are extremely bad-tempered!

Moments later there was a growling, snarling, spitting ball of monsters scrapping over the table. Claws snipped, spines snapped, pits squirted, horns butted and the 'eye' monsters pulled each other's hair very aggressively.

Will saw the table creaking under their weight and shot beneath the cloth. He hooked his forks under Urk's rucksack and yanked him free, just as the table collapsed with an almighty *CRASH*! The heap of fighting monsters paused for a second and then continued the battle, rolling around in the mess of food in a frenzied ball of fury.

'Let's get out of here!' Urk and Will gasped together.

They legged it away from Monster

Hall, and kept on legging it until they could no longer hear the growls and roars from the scrapping monsters – a long way away on the outskirts of Monster City.

'How did you know they'd fall for that?' asked Will as Urk dropped the bottles one by one into a murky, gurgling river with pongflies buzzing over the surface. 'They could have just lifted the tablecloth!'

PONGFLIES

Fat monster flies who feast on filth.

'Monsters are pretty hot-headed,' said Urk, 'They snip, squirt and squash now and ask questions later. Most don't even bother asking questions later – they just keep snipping, squirting and squashing.'

'But what about tomorrow?' said Will. 'They'll all be at my school!'

'Oh, they won't turn up without the Stink Ink!' said Urk. 'Disappointing a giant like Pongdollop usually means getting eaten – even if he's supposed to be a vegetarian. And I'll bet most of them only turned up for the free food anyway.'

'Pongdollop will still turn up, though,' said Will. 'And he's got his own whiffy pus-sacks all ready to squirt!'

'Well, at least you'll have a ringside seat!' laughed Urk, as the last of the bottles burped into the oozy depths.

'I still can't believe you suggested your *own school* for the putrid apocalypse.'

'That was pretty dumb,' sighed Will. 'But I guess this way I'll be able to keep an eye out for him, and maybe even have a go at trying to stop him.'

'What did you say?' Urk frowned.

'I know,' Will sighed. 'How could *I* stop the great and mighty Pongdollop?'

'No, what did you say before that?'

'Keep an eye out for him?'

Urk took a seat on the bank of
the smelly river and flicked through
the 'Ghastly Gadgets' section of the
Monsterbook.

'Aha!' he said eventually.
'I *knew* there was
something weird
about him.'
'I thought
everything about
him was weird,'

said Will, sitting down and adjusting his sacking. 'Not to mention violent!'

'Did you notice one of Pongdollop's eyes was all yellow and swirly?' asked Urk. 'Like it was a bit more evil than the other three?'

'Um, yeah, I guess so,' said Will, recalling the terrifying close-up he got when Pongdollop bore down on him. 'I thought it was just a monster thing – you know, one eye, ten eyes, yellow swirly eye . . .'

'That last one was an *Evil Eye!*' said Urk, pointing to the page in the book.

EVIL EYES

Evil Eyes are very popular among the lazier, less ambitious monsters. Each eyeball takes a year to make, but if the lazy lump can wait that long, he'll be filled with pure evil!

Here please!

Tum-tee-tum

GRRRRRRRR!

Always pop your Evil Eye into a glass at night to charge up the evil.

HOOVER-HEADS

If you don't already have an empty socket, eye-eating Hoover-Heads will offer their sucky services for free!

we suck

so you don't have to

'At least we know why Pongdollop's not a big lazy lump,' said Will, closing the *Monsterbook* and handing it back. 'But

knowing about the eye doesn't really help us, does it?'

'It does if we can steal the Evil Eye out from under his nose,' said Urk. 'Or was the eye above his nose? Where was his nose?'

'I don't think he had a nose,' said Will.

'Either way, without the Evil Eye he'll turn back into a big lazy lump,' said Urk, packing the *Monsterbook* away in his rucksack. 'And then he won't even care about the uprising any more.'

'But how will we get our hands on it?' asked Will. 'It's next to three other eyes that can all see properly. So I'm thinking we can't exactly sneak up on him!'

'The *Monsterbook* says he'll be keeping the Evil Eye in a glass tonight. That's our one chance to steal it and stop the uprising!' Urk jumped up and pulled Will to his feet. 'But we need to go back to my place first to do some research.'

'Won't your parents be there?' said Will, hurrying after Urk as he led them through a series of dark alleyways. Will

tried not to notice the various shapes,
sizes and numbers of eyes peering out
at them from the shadows.

'I hope not,' said Urk, ducking into a
stairwell.

Halfway up a mudblock named Terror Towers, the monster opened one of the many brown doors, poked his head inside and looked around carefully. Then he pressed a finger to his lips and ushered Will inside.

MUDBLOCK
Monsterland is very highly populated, so many monsters live in mudblocks – high-rise housing made from dried mud.

The pair tiptoed down a small hallway and slipped into the first room on the right. Once inside, Urk closed the door quietly and hurried to the bookshelf. He pulled down a large brown book and heaved it over to the bed.

'What's that?' asked Will, joining Urk as he began flicking through the index.

'The *Brown Pages*,' said Urk. 'We need
to find out where Pongdollop is staying.
He's from the Outer Regions so he'll be
holed up in a hotel somewhere, and there
aren't many with rooms *that* size.'

Will looked around Urk's bedroom
and found it was similar to his own in size
and furniture. Except everything in this
room was made of mud and rags and it
smelled quite bad.

Urk tore a page from the *Brown Pages* and handed it to Will.

✣ **THE GOLIATH** ✣

Catering to Monsterland's more
generously proportioned visitors!

SUPERSIZED TOILETS!   INFINITY WALLOW!
CRANE-LIFT TO ALL FLOORS!

✣ **THE GIGANTICA SUITE** ✣

FOR THE LARGEST OF THE LARGE!

In town to gather monster minions for a
mass scare? Book our Gigantica Suite
for a great pre-fright nap!

7
Miffni the Big

'URRRRRRK!' roared an angry voice from the hallway. 'IS THAT YOU, SNEAKING AROUND LIKE A LITTLE BOGEY BUG?'

Urk snatched the page back and quickly slipped it into the *Monsterbook*. Suddenly, the door burst open and a much larger version of himself filled the doorway with a very angry look

BOGEY BUG

Tiny green bugs that live in larger monster nostrils.

on its face. Will noticed it was wearing
lipstick, which was the only clue that this
monster might be a girl.

'Oh, you've brought a little friend
home!' she sneered.

'Yeah,' said Urk. 'So what?'

'That's a first!' she chuckled spitefully.

'Well, aren't you going to introduce us?'

'Willijub, this is my sister Miffni,' said Urk. 'Miffni, this is Willijub.'

Urk's sister snorted an unfriendly greeting while Will waved a friendly fork.

'Where are Mum and Dad?' asked Urk, keen to draw attention away from Will.

'They're out on scare manoeuvres, of course!' snapped Miffni.

'Well, we're just going out again,' said Urk, grabbing the *Monsterbook* and

standing up. Will
got up too, but
Miffni pursed
her lips, folded
her arms and
showed no
intention of
budging.

'Where are you going?' she asked,
narrowing her eyes.

'Mind your own business,' said Urk.

'If you don't tell me where you're
going, you're not going anywhere,'
she growled and then shifted to fill as
much of the doorway as she could –
which was all of it. 'I'm the biggest,
so I'm in charge when Mum and Dad
aren't here!'

'If you don't move I'll get my friend

to show you a leg!' threatened Urk.

'You wouldn't *dare*!' Miffni hissed,
eyeing Will and her brother nervously.

Urk snorted and tried to look fearless,
which wasn't easy, knowing that if she
called his bluff, Will would be showing
her a leg in jeans with a muddy trainer
on the end.

'Oh, I don't care what you're doing
anyway!' Miffni huffed. 'It's probably

something *really* stupid and boring!'
And with this she stomped off down
the hallway mumbling to herself.

'Phew!' sighed Urk, as they hurried
from the mudblock and back on to the
street. 'That was close!'

'I didn't know you had a big sister,'
said Will.

'Oh, she's not my *big* sister,' Urk
explained. 'She's my *little* sister, who
just happens to be really big. We don't
get on at all.'

Urk led them to what Will decided was
a more upmarket district of Monster City.
The streets were lined with giant curly
dog-poo-style buildings and they were all
bigger and more elaborate than Monster
Hall. The monsters they passed also
seemed to be more important-looking.

Some were being ferried along the street by several straining Underlings, while others had a single Underling

perched on their heads, holding an umbrella. Will thought this was odd for lots of reasons, but mostly because it wasn't raining.

'WEE WEE!' yelled a voice above them.

Will glanced up in time to see a large bucket appear through a high window before Urk bundled him into the nearest doorway. Moments later a jet of steaming liquid hit the pavement with an enormous *SPLOSH*!

'Not *all* the hotels have toilets,' Urk explained, as they stepped around the steaming puddle and continued down the street. 'Just in case you were wondering about the umbrellas.'

MONSTER TOILETS

Toilets are an exciting new addition to Monsterland, even though they still have no plumbing. When it's flushed, the monster waste is carried away in wheelbarrows and used to feed the Fungus Forest.

Not surprisingly, The Goliath was the
biggest of all the giant curly dog-poo-style
buildings. In fact, it looked like several
giant curly dog poos arranged into a large
pooey pyramid. Urk was about to stroll

casually into the foyer when Will leapt
in front of him, waving his forks in alarm.

'We're not just going to walk in there,
are we?' he whispered urgently. 'I thought
we might sneak in or something?'

'We will sneak in, but we have to find
the room first,' Urk explained. 'Anyway,
we're part of the great and mighty
Pongdollop's uprising, so we're kind of
allowed to be here.'

Will stepped aside and followed Urk
into the building, where he found the
foyer was much more fancy than
Monster Hall. Fanciness in Monsterland
amounted to straw on the floor, *carved*
dung ceilings and ploppy chandeliers
with extra-big plops.

A small stripy monster sat behind
the reception desk with a spray of thin
tentacles writhing
around her head,
each strand
busying itself
with various
filing tasks.

Will could tell the creature was a 'her' because, like Miffni, she had a smudge of lipstick across her mouth.

'Yessss?' she hissed, three beady eyes peering over the desk.

'We're here to see the great and mighty Pongdollop,' Urk stated confidently.

'Are you expected?' she demanded, a tentacle shooting behind her and poking around inside a pigeonhole labelled THE GIGANTICA SUITE.

She pulled out a scrap of paper with 'DOONT DYSTEERB' scribbled in a familiar Pongdollopy scrawl and waved it at him.

'Er, not exactly,' said Urk. 'But we have very important news about tomorrow's gloriously disgusting plot to take over the world. Mr Pongdollop

will *definitely* want to see us.'

The tentacles on the receptionist's
head paused for a moment while she
considered this, then they wiggled in
the direction of the stairs.

'Top floor,' she said curtly. 'The crane-
lift has a weight *minimum*.'

'What's the plan
once we get there?'
asked Will as they made their way up
the damp winding staircase. Grubby
light bulbs flickered on the walls, buzzing
angrily whenever the damp trickled
too close.

'Snatch the Evil Eye, of course,' replied
Urk.

'Just like that?' said Will.

'I guess so,' Urk shrugged, running through the plan in his head. 'We know Pongdollop doesn't want to be *dysteerbed*, so he's probably getting a good night's sleep before the big day.'

'And if he's not?' asked Will.

Urk paused on the stair as though he hadn't considered the possibility of Pongdollop not being asleep and gave Will a worried look. 'Let's just *really* hope he is,' he said.

8
Snoring and Spearing

There was no question whether
Pongdollop was asleep or not when
they reached the
Gigantica Suite.
The whole floor
was rumbling and
vibrating with the
sound of snoring.
There was a
giant door at
the top of
the stairs,

with what looked like a large walnut sleeping beside it.

'I'd forgotten about him!' whispered Urk.

'Me too,' whispered Will.

The pair crept forward, watching the sleeping Underling the whole time, then they slid the door back and slipped into the room. The sound of snoring inside was almost deafening.

The Gigantica Suite was hot and gloomy with extra-large everything. In the centre lay a giant mattress with Pongdollop sprawled across it, his bottom lip flapping with each clattering snore.

'There it is!' gasped Urk, pointing to the edge of the mattress.

On the floor beside the sleeping

Octapongus sat a small glass of murky
liquid. Through the murk they saw a
swirly yellow eyeball. It was giving evil
looks to everything in the room.

Urk took a deep breath, tiptoed
forward, and was about to grab the glass
when the spotty mountain of monster
made a great snuffling sound. Suddenly,
Pongdollop tumbled over like a rolling

landslide and the little monster leapt
back as a sleep-slithering tentacle
scooped up the glass.

Urk and Will froze and watched with
horror as a single eyelid slowly opened.

Luckily, the eyelid was the second
from the left, so there was nothing

inside but a big black hole. It twitched a
couple of times and then closed again as
the monster resumed snoring.

'What do we do now?' Will gasped,
looking at the glass held firmly in the
tentacle's grip. Urk was
watching the glass
too, but his eyes
had glazed
over and his
mouth had

dropped open in fright. Will knew it was
up to him to get his hands on the eye.

'And all I have are forks,' he sighed, and
then raised a curious eyebrow.

Will crept forward and peered into the
glass, where the Evil Eye bobbed up and
down like a pickled
onion in a jar
of vinegar, then
he lifted a fork
and speared it
with one well-
aimed jab.

'Urgh!' he
shuddered,
peering at the yellow squidgy ball.

Creeping away from the sleeping
monster, Will quickly steered the zombie
Urk out of the Gigantica Suite. He closed

the door and sighed heavily, relieved
to have the Evil Eye and that his friend
had closed his mouth and was blinking
again.

'We did it!' Will whispered, waving
the eye triumphantly. 'We *actually* did it!'

'You actually did what?' said a raspy
voice at their feet.

Will and Urk
looked down at the
yawning Underling.
The Underling
looked at Will,
then he looked at
Urk, and finally
he looked at the
Evil Eye on the end of Will's fork. His
own beady eyes grew larger as he pieced
it all together.

Will quickly whipped the fork behind
his back, but it was too late.

'MASTER!' yelled the Underling,
scrabbling for the door.

Will and Urk bolted down the spiral
stairs three at a time, the floors of the
hotel whizzing by in a blur of panic. When
they eventually hit the foyer, the pair

screeched to a halt and sauntered casually past the reception desk.

'Thank you,' said Urk, waving at the receptionist.

'Lovely hotel,' added Will.

Back on the street they started running again, and they kept running until they reached the edge of Monster City. There they slowed to a fast walk through the Fungus Forest and back into the tunnels.

The moment he stepped from the wardrobe into his room, Will flicked away the forks, threw off the rag and scratched his itchy head like a fleabag dog. Everything around him looked *really* bright and clean compared to the mucky murkiness of Monsterland.

MONSTERLAND

After a short time in Monsterland, a fleshblob would quickly get used to the gloom, filth and smell. This makes the world of fleshblobs appear hideously bright and clean.

'Phew!' he sighed. 'I can't believe we just did that!'

'Stealing the eye?' said Urk, picking up the fork with Pongdollop's Evil Eye

harpooned on the end and frowning at
the swirly evilness. Something was
troubling him, but he couldn't put his
finger on exactly what.

'No, saving the world!' Will gasped.
'We just saved the world from a mad
smelly monster!'

'Yeah, I guess we did,' said Urk,
popping the eye into his rucksack. 'Don't

you think it was a bit *easy*, though?'

Will considered everything they'd
been through in the last couple of hours,
including Big Ugly Jennie spit on his
head and dog-poo buildings and a roaring
Octapongus and scrapping buffets and
massive sisters and wee-wee dodging
and eyeball kebabs . . .

'No,' he said eventually. 'I don't think
it was easy *at all*.'

'I don't mean that,'
said Urk. 'I just think

it's a bit strange that all we had to do was nab the Evil Eye, then Pongdollop waddles back to the Outer Regions and we've saved the school from a smelly uprising.'

'Well, we're OK for about a year,' said Will. 'That's how long the *Monsterbook* said it takes to make an Evil Eye, assuming Pongdollop can be bothered to wait that long again.'

'But why did he wait that long in the first place?' said Urk. 'Octapongi are meant to be lazy.'

'Maybe he got bored?' Will suggested.

'I guess so,' said Urk, pulling on his rucksack and heading for the wardrobe. 'Same time tomorrow, then?'

'You bring the book and I'll bring the crisps,' said Will.

The boy watched as Urk
disappeared through the hidden
doorway, then he closed the
door, kicked off his muddy
trainers and
collapsed on to
the bed. A very
short time
later he was
fast asleep.

9

'Psssssst!'

Will was tired the next day at school. He was also very bored with how normal everything was after the excitement of his adventure in Monsterland. At break time he sat on a bench and watched his classmates, feeling quite proud that he'd stopped Pongdollop from squirting them all with Stink Ink.

'Psssssst!' said a voice beside him.

Will looked around, saw nothing and decided his late night was making him imagine things.

'PSSSSST!!!' said the voice again, but louder this time.

Will looked closer and saw a pair of eyes peering out at him from the gap in the litterbin.

LITTERBINS

Litterbins make a very handy hidden doorway for use during the day. Ninety per cent of litterbins have a tunnel beneath them. Fleshblobs never look inside and they're refreshingly smelly.

He leapt back with an embarrassingly high-pitched squeal.

'It's me!' whispered a familiar voice. 'Urk.'

Will quickly took a seat next to the bin and tried to look casual.

'What are you doing here?' he hissed. 'Someone might see you.'

'We're in trouble!' said Urk, pushing the *Monsterbook* through the gap in the bin. Will glanced around the playground to make sure no one was looking before he took it.

'Look at the "Evil Eye" section,' said Urk.

'We read that last night,' said Will, flicking through.

'Yeah, I thought so too,' said Urk. 'But I was so sure we'd missed something that I read it again this morning and found something important.'

Will found the page and quickly scanned the text.

'What?' he said. 'I can't see anything different . . .'

'The *small* print at the bottom,' said Urk.

Will lifted the book up to his face and was about to say 'What small print?' when he found a few lines of tiny text that at first glance looked like a smudge at the bottom of the page.

> Most Evil Eye manufacturers will provide you with a spare Evil Eye as they are easily lost or stolen.
> Do not be tempted to wear more than one Evil Eye for extra evilness! Wearing multiple Evil Eyes is very dangerous!

'Uh oh!' said Will, lowering the book and scanning the playground.

It was then that he noticed something odd, or rather *someone* odd. There was a strange woman walking through the school gate, and she was holding the hand of a girl in a very large bonnet.

Will couldn't decide why the

woman looked so odd, until she waddled
into the playground and he noticed that
one of her eyes was yellow and swirly and
very evil-looking!

'How do you think Pongdollop will get
to the surface?' Will asked the litterbin.

FLESHBLOB SUITS

lifelike
rubber
skin

handy
hanger

voice
box

head
mask

Fleshblob suits are a very realistic human disguise. They were invented to allow monsters to sneak around above ground and scare fleshblob children during the day when they least expect it.

TOAD FAT & SHRIVEL SALTS

Most monsters are larger than humans and lather themselves in Toad Fat to squeeze into a fleshblob suit. Giant monsters have to actually shrink their bodies using Shrivel Salts!

'Er, he'll probably shrivel down
and squeeze into a rubber fleshblob suit,'
said Urk. 'Why do you ask?'

'Because I'm pretty sure he's already
here!' said Will, nodding towards the
woman and the girl. 'We have to find a
way to clear the playground!'

'That I can do,'
said Urk, and began
climbing out through
the gap in the litterbin.

'What are you
doing?' Will
gasped.

'Clearing the
playground.'

'But everyone will see you!'

'That's the plan,' said Urk, brushing
crisp bags and sweet wrappers from his

shoulders and flicking an apple core off his head. 'It's better they see me than *smell* the great and mighty Pongdollop!'

Urk arched his head back, opened his

mouth as wide as it would go and then roared at the top of his voice. It was a very impressive roar, especially coming from such a small monster.

Everyone in the playground froze, looked around, and then stampeded into the school, shrieking and screaming and waving their arms. It reminded Will of a bad monster movie, one where a crowd runs away from a giant killer turnip.

'Wow!' he said enthusiastically. Until
he realized they were now alone in
the playground with
the angry-looking
Pongdollop lady and the
peculiar girl, who
looked suspiciously
Underling-shaped!

10
Lady Balloon Head

The Underling skipped over to the school fountain, pressed a finger over the spout and sent a jet of water across the playground towards the Pongdollop lady.

Under the flow of water Pongdollop's rubber mask began to swell like a balloon, stretching the features like a freaky fairground mirror. The head balloon expanded to twice the size of the body before the rubber finally burst with a *BANG!* Pongdollop's massive head popped out and wobbled above the tiny body – a

tiny body wearing a dress and holding a handbag.

'GRRRR!' growled Pongdollop, waving his handbag at Will and Urk.

Moments later, the body began to make squelchy noises as it too began swelling and swaying and eventually toppled over. Like a beetle on its back, the arms and legs wiggled, growing longer and fatter until each one pinged into the air like fleshy rubber bands. Pongdollop had tucked two tentacles into each limb, and they now writhed wildly, swelling and lifting him upright.

The Underling child abandoned the fountain, threw off his pink dress and the bonnet that hid the hump, and scuttled across the playground. He leapt on to one of Pongdollop's tentacles and scaled the side of the monster's head. There he

whispered something into a giant crusty hole.

'*YOU* STOLE MY EVIL EYE?' roared Pongdollop, glaring at Will and Urk.

The pair exchanged panicked glances.

'What do we do now?' yelled Will.

'RUN!' yelled Urk.

Charging across the playground, Will led them round to the back of the school. He wasn't sure where he was going, and he wasn't sure he cared as long as it was away from Pongdollop!

Pongdollop charged after them with the Underling perched on his head, shouting encouragement. The octapongus was roaring and growling and gaining on them very quickly, so Will grabbed Urk's arm and dragged him through the double doors of the canteen. It was too early for the canteen staff to be preparing for lunch and the only place in the school with no kids to get squirted.

Pongdollop tried to follow them and knocked the Underling flying as he attempted to squeeze his fat head through the door. He got halfway through and then became wedged in the doorframe, which made him even angrier.

'GRRRR!' he growled, inching himself further into the canteen with a series of energetic thrusts and grunts. His body

made horrible squelchy sounds as it
squidged through the hole.

'I didn't think he'd get through that
gap,' gasped Will.

'Well, at least it's slowed him down,'
said Urk, grabbing the *Monsterbook* and
flicking through it frantically. The young
monster returned to the 'Evil Eye' page
and scratched his head. Will saw another

smudge below the small print that looked
like *more* small print, but on closer
inspection it was just a smudge.

Urk was thinking about Evil Eyes and
suddenly remembered a cautionary tale
the little monsters were told in Basic Boo.
He quickly went to the 'Horrible History'
section of the book until he found what
he wanted.

THE LESSON OF LILILUMP

· —————— ·

Lililump was one of our most beloved monsters, achieving over a thousand wet mattresses in her lifetime. But her glorious career was cut short by the use of multiple Evil Eyes!

Being a Deccapeep, Lililump decided to experiment with nine evil eyes – leaving only one real eye to see through! The overload of evil sent Lililump on a rampage through Monster City, until she eventually collapsed in a heap with smoke billowing from her blowhole.

11
Stinky Squirty Showdown

Just as they finished reading 'The Lesson of Lililump', Pongdollop burst through the door with a massive grunt. The Underling scuttled after him, red-faced and exhausted from shoving his master's bottom from the other side.

Pongdollop slithered to the centre of the canteen while Urk and Will backed away until they hit the wall. The Octapongus gave a jagged sneer as

he rose up on two tentacles, bearing his
entire underbelly.

'YUCK!' said Will, waving a hand in
front of his nose as the odour filled his
nostrils. 'What on earth are *those*?'

Dangling from Pongdollop's underbelly
were eight black sacks that throbbed and
steamed, giving off a putrid stench that

would make the filthiest
skunk blush with
embarrassment.

'Those are his pus-sacks!' coughed Urk,
choking on the fumes.

STINK ETIQUETTE

Monsters are not immune to
the putrid concoctions other
monsters can stew in their
pus-sacks and pit-pumps.
Accidental firing of these
body-pistols can cause great
offence, so there are corks
and plugs you can buy to
avoid embarrassment.

'Cower before me, puny fleshblob
and traitor monster!' Pongdollop
boomed, bobbing up and down to pump
up the pus-sacks before aiming them
straight at Will and Urk.

Urk threw the book down and
rummaged in the rucksack behind his
back.

'Are you any good at throwing?' he
whispered to Will.

'Um, I'm OK, I guess,' Will frowned.
'But I think we have more important
things to worry about at the moment!'

Urk passed him the Evil Eye behind
his back.

'You only have one shot!' the monster
whispered gravely. 'And you need to
get it in the Evil Eye socket. Then he'll
be wearing two and hopefully his head

will explode or something!'

'Are you sure it won't just make him twice as evil?' asked Will. 'Because he's pretty evil already and I don't want to make him worse.'

'Have you got a better idea?' Urk shrugged.

Will didn't have a better idea, so he swallowed hard and sized up the weight of the squidgy eyeball in his hand. The feel

of the eye and the stench of Pongdollop's
pus-sacks made him feel quite queasy, but
he tried to concentrate.

He focused on the Evil Eye that was
now glaring at him.

'WHAT'S THAT!' roared Pongdollop,
flexing all eight pus-sacks until they
swivelled round and pointed directly at
the boy.

'What's what?' asked Will innocently.

'The traitor monster gave you something!' he snarled. 'I want to see it!'

'You want to see it?' said Will.

'YES!' growled Pongdollop.

'Are you sure?'

'I *DEMAND* TO SEE –' boomed Pongdollop, but he didn't get to finish before Will swung his arm wide and lobbed the squidgy eyeball with all his might at the monster.

Will and Urk watched in slow motion
as the yellow swirly eye sailed through the
air towards Pongdollop. But he lurched
back at the last minute and the eyeball
stuck firmly in his crusty right earhole!

'Uh oh!' said Will and Urk at the same
time.

Pongdollop frowned, twitched and tilted his head as the Evil Eye swivelled in his ear. Then he glared at Urk and Will with three regular eyes, the spare Evil Eye second on the left, and the peculiar evil *ear* eye on the right.

The Octapongus looked very odd, but also definitely more evil than before, twice as evil in fact.

'HA! HA! HA!' he boomed as the extra evil swirled around his brain.

Pongdollop bobbed up and down
again like a grim jelly, aimed his pus-sacks
at Will and Urk, squeezed hard – and
then slumped in a big fat smelly heap.
A small ring of smoke rose from the
empty earhole on the left.

'Squirt them, master! Squirt them
now!' yelled the Underling as he scuttled
up Pongdollop's back and on to his head.

The Underling peered down at the
fallen dribbling monster, plucked out the
two Evil Eyes and sighed heavily. Then
he glared at the stupid expression on
Pongdollop's face and stamped his foot
angrily on his head.

'ARRRRRGGGGH!' growled the
Underling.

Will and Urk
exchanged
confused
glances.

'Do you know
how long it took
me to turn this
BIG STUPID LUMP
into something
great and
mighty?'
he yelled,
jumping up
and down
with fury on Pongdollop's sleeping head.

'You?' Will and Urk said together.

'YES, ME!' roared the Underling. 'This
USELESS HEAP couldn't even wipe his
own bottom before I came along, he was
. . .' The Underling thought about it for a
moment and then got very angry again.
'. . . He was just like this! A DROOLING,
DRIBBLING BLOB!'

'HA! HA! HA!' laughed Will and
Urk together, and Pongdollop looked
pretty happy too, in a dumb, dribbly
kind of way.

The Underling rolled his eyes,
scuttled down the nearest tentacle and
disappeared into the storeroom of the
canteen. He returned moments later
with a large tub of salt and began circling
the fallen monster,
shaking the salt all
over him.

'What are you doing?' asked Will.

'Well, I won't get him home *this* size, will I?' he grumbled, as Pongdollop began to shrink. His tentacles shrivelled inwards and his massive head went down like a wrinkled balloon.

'That's how the big monsters get into fleshblob suits,' whispered Urk. 'They're mostly made of water and the salt makes them shrink.'

When Pongdollop had shrivelled to a manageable size, the Underling heaved a tentacle over his shoulder and dragged the shrunken Octapongus across the canteen, leaving a wet slimy trail along the floor.

'Don't think this is the end of it!' he panted, straining with the weight. 'In a couple of years I'll have him looking

great and mighty again, then you two
had better *watch out*!'

And with this the Underling and the
saggy Pongdollop disappeared into the
nearest hidden doorway, which was
conveniently located behind a large
potted fern in the corner of the canteen.

12
Mad Monster Dog

That night, Urk stepped from the
wardrobe and plonked his rucksack on
Will's cluttered desk.

'BOO!' he said.

'ARGH!' said Will, glancing up from
the newspaper. 'What's up?'

'I'm glad to say nothing,' smiled Urk.
'You?'

'Something even *more* terrifying
than Pongdollop!' warned Will, and
read the headline from the newspaper
aloud. '"FEROCIOUS MAD DOG

TERRORIZES CHILDREN!",' he said
with a worried look on his face.

'And you think this "MAD DOG" is a
monster?' said Urk.

'I'm not sure; they've done an artist's
impression from the description given by
the witnesses.' Will grinned, holding up
the paper for Urk to see. But it wasn't
yesterday's *Nasty News*, it was the local
evening newspaper from that day.

THE
EVENING NEWS

FEROCIOUS
MAD DOG
TERRORIZES CHILDREN!

St Margaret's Elementary School was terrorized today by a rabid mad dog believed to be roaming the neighbourhood!

Witnesses said that it had massive teeth and was completely ferocious and scary!

(full story on page 7)

'My parents *will* be proud!' said Urk.
And they both burst out laughing.

ASK MICHAEL!

'Of all the books you've written, which one is your favourite?'

My favourite book is *Pongdollop and the School Stink* because it was my first adventure with Urk and Will. I really like that they're both from completely different worlds but are still the best of friends. Pongdollop the Monster was also great fun to write because he's so big and angry and smelly.

'If you couldn't be an author, what would you like to be?'

I would probably be an artist. I like to paint in my spare time and the pictures usually have loads of things going on in them. This way I'd still be able to make up characters and tell stories, and get really messy.

'What's the best thing about writing stories?'

The best thing about writing stories is that there are no limits. You can make absolutely anything happen, all you have to do is imagine it. *Monsterbook* is particularly fun because I get to imagine a whole underground world filled with very strange creatures.

'Your characters have all sorts of incredible adventures – what's the most amazing thing that happened to you at school?'

Nothing very amazing happened at my school. We never had a Werewolf Teacher or a Robot Dinner Lady (that I know of). Sometimes a stray dog would wander into the playground, which was always very exciting. The rest of the time I spent wondering what would happen if alien spaceships landed. I still do!

puffin.co.uk

Read all the unbelievable adventures of

JAKE CAKE

that's me ↑

I did all the writing and all the drawing

puffin.co.uk

Puffin Books

Why should your eyes have all the fun?

Give your ears a treat and hear your favourite classics come to life!

Go to the Puffin Podcast on the all-new **puffin.co.uk** now!

Celebrity podcasters include Eoin Colfer, Meg Rosoff, Darren Shan and Garth Nix.

Hear Captain Hook in action, *listen* to Long John Silver, enjoy the *sound* of the Psammead and much, much more!

puffin.co.uk